Agnes Under the Big Top

A TALL TALE

by Aditi Brennan Kapil

A SAMUEL FRENCH ACTING EDITION

FOUNDED 1830

SAMUELFRENCH.COM

MUSIC USE NOTE

Licensees are solely responsible for obtaining formal written permission from copyright owners to use copyrighted music in the performance of this play and are strongly cautioned to do so. If no such permission is obtained by the licensee, then the licensee must use only original music that the licensee owns and controls. Licensees are solely responsible and liable for all music clearances and shall indemnify the copyright owners of the play and their licensing agent, Samuel French, Inc., against any costs, expenses, losses and liabilities arising from the use of music by licensees.

IMPORTANT BILLING AND CREDIT
REQUIREMENTS

All producers of *AGNES UNDER THE BIG TOP must* give credit to the Author of the Play in all programs distributed in connection with performances of the Play, and in all instances in which the title of the Play appears for the purposes of advertising, publicizing or otherwise exploiting the Play and/or a production. The name of the Author *must* appear on a separate line on which no other name appears, immediately following the title and *must* appear in size of type not less than fifty percent of the size of the title type.

In addition the following credit *must* be given in all programs and publicity information distributed in association with this piece:

**Originally commissioned and produced by the
Mixed Blood Theatre Company of Minneapolis, MN.**

Agnes Under the Big Top **was developed through a consortium led by The Lark Play Development Center (New York City) and includes Rhodopi International Theatre Lab (Smolyan, Bulgaria), Interact Theatre (Philadelphia), Mixed Blood Theatre Company (Minneapolis), and The Playwrights' Center (Minneapolis).**

Agnes Under the Big Top **was selected as an NEA Distinguished New Play Development Project as part of the NEA New Play Development Program, Hosted by Arena Stage."**

AGNES UNDER THE BIG TOP was commissioned by Mixed Blood Theatre, and selected as a NEA Distinguished New Play Development Project as part of the NEA New Play Development Program, hosted by Arena Stage. The play was developed through a consortium led by The Lark Play Development Center (New York City) and includes Rhodopi International Theatre Lab (Smolyan, Bulgaria), Interact Theatre (Philadelphia), and Mixed Blood Theatre Company (Minneapolis) and The Playwrights' Center (Minneapolis).

Aditi Kapil (playwright) and Liz Engelman (dramaturg) were participants in the TCG/ITI Travel Grants program, funded by the Trust for Mutual Understanding and administered by Theatre Communications Group, the national organization for the American theatre.

The world premiere of *AGNES UNDER THE BIG TOP* was presented in a National New Play Network rolling world premiere at Mixed Blood Theatre (MN), Long Wharf Theatre (CT), and Borderlands Theatre (AZ).

The play opened at The Mixed Blood Theatre (Jack Reuler, Artistic Director) in Minneapolis, MN on February 18, 2011. It was directed by Aditi Kapil, assisted by Rebekah Rentzel, with scenic design by Andrea Heilman, lighting by Jeff Bartlett, sound by Katherine Horowitz, costumes by Amber Brown, and dramaturgy by Liz Engelman. The stage manager was Ashley Warren. The cast was as follows:

AGNES	Shá Cage
ELLA	Linda Kelsey
ROZA	Virginia S. Burke
SHIPKOV	Nathaniel Fuller
HAPPY	Ankit Dogra
BUSKER	Nick Demeris

The play opened at Long Wharf Theatre (Gordon Edelstein, Artistic Director) in New Haven, CT on March 9, 2011. It was directed by Eric Ting, with scenic design by Frank Alberino, lighting by Tyler Micoleau, sound by Katie Down, costumes by Jessica Wegener Shay, and dialect diesign by Amy Stoller. The stage manager was Megan Schwartz Dickert. The cast was as follows:

AGNES	Francesca Choy-Kee
ELLA	Laura Esterman
ROZA	Gergana Mellin
SHIPKOV	Michael Cullen
HAPPY	Eshan Bay
BUSKER	Sam Ghosh

The play opened at Borderlands Theatre in Tucson, AZ (Barclay Goldsmith, Artistic Director) on February 9, 2012. It was directed by Barclay Goldsmith, with scenic design by John Longhoffre, lighting by Clint Bryson, sound by Kim Klingenfus, and costumes by Kathy Hurst. The stage manager was Eza Tessler. the cast was as follows:

AGNES	T Loving
ELLA	Toni Press-Coffman
ROZA	Susan Arnold
SHIPKOV	Philip Bennett
HAPPY	Laxmi Dahal
BUSKER	Brian Taraz

CHARACTERS

AGNES - Liberian immigrant, 30s, Ella's home care worker. Tough and funny.

ELLA - American, white. A rheumatoid, bedridden woman. She is deformed and wooden, her fingers trapped in claws. Prematurely aged.

ROZA - Bulgarian immigrant, 40s, speaks Bulgarian, Ella's home care worker. Silent except when addressing birds.

SHIPKOV - Bulgarian immigrant, 40s, Roza's husband, drives a subway train. Former ringmaster.

HAPPY - Indian, 20s, recently immigrated con artist, training as subway driver. Smiles a lot.

BUSKER - Plays an instrument on the subway platform, is all other voices/voiceovers, moves freely through time and space

SET PIECES

a bed
a subway train
a pole
windows, doors, and seats

All the characters inhabit the same apartment set when necessary, the one permanently occupied by Ella. The window is a shared window.

ALTERNATE ENDING

For productions that are unable to, or choose not to, position Shipkov on top of his subway train for scene 23, an alternate scene 23 text is available, following the text of the play.

ACKNOWLEDGEMENTS

The playwright would like to thank the following people for their invaluable contributions to this play:

My parents Satish Kapil and Ivanka Kapil for the use of their stories.

My cousin Happy Kapil, and my aunt Roza Zlateva, for the use of their names.

My artistic teams at the NEA, Arena Stage, Lark Play Development Center, Mixed Blood Theatre, Interact Theatre, The Rhodopi International Theatre Laboratory, The Playwrights' Center, The National New Play Network, Long Wharf Theatre, Borderlands Theatre, and in particular Liz Engelman, Eric Ting, and Antje Oegel, for journeying with Agnes as she found story.

My children Vyara, Nadezhda, and Stefan, for allowing me to tell them tall tales.

And always, my husband Sean.

1

(in the dark)

ANNOUNCER VO. …stand back from the doors as the train approaches the terminal. Please stand back from the doors as the train approaches the terminal. Terminal. Do you hear me? Agnes? Agnes.

*(Sound of subway doors opening as lights reveal **AGNES** sitting in a chair.)*

(This is a quiet place.)

AGNES. I heard you.

I'm late.

DOCTOR VO. You understand that there's nothing/

AGNES. Nothing that you can do, it's finished, yes I understand. Got it.

DOCTOR VO. You're terminal.

AGNES. Sure. Aren't we all.

DOCTOR VO. It's a matter of weeks. I don't like to estimate… One can never be absolutely sure with cancer.

AGNES. No schedule?

DOCTOR VO. No exact schedule, no

AGNES. But then how do I know when to arrive at the station?

DOCTOR VO. Excuse me?

AGNES. The station? When I need to arrive at the station? Terminal.

It's a joke.

DOCTOR VO. I'm sorry

AGNES. Well, I should get back to work

DOCTOR VO. When you're ready to talk to someone about
your further care, I'll connect you with/

AGNES. Maybe later

(Sound of subway doors shutting as lights crossfade.)

2

(The subway platform)

(A **BUSKER** *plays in the background, barely audible.)*

*(***HAPPY** *is looking at his cellphone.)*

*(***AGNES** *stares out, immobile for several long beats.)*

(This is a loud place.)

HAPPY. Shit!

*(***AGNES** *looks at him.)*

Sorry… no signal down here! It's crazy, right?

*(***AGNES** *doesn't respond.)*

(Silence)

(Sound of train arriving at the station, the announcer is garbled.)

ANNOUNCER VO. This is the blue line, eastbound, please stand back from the doors. Blue line, eastbound.

(Sound of subway doors opening, lights shift.)

3

(Ella's apartment)

*(**ELLA** speaks briskly on the phone.)*

*(**ROZA** is gathering her things to leave.)*

*(**AGNES** enters.)*

(This is a quiet place.)

ELLA. –if I have another episode they're going to try a different medication, but they're concerned about combining with, anyway all the other medicines are working fine, my hands aren't better, of course the arthritis hasn't improved in thirty years why would my hands be better, the point is managing the diabetes, ok if you're not going to pick up I can just stop talking.

Fine.

Fine.

You said you were interested.

When are you coming by?

Good bye, Frederick.

*(**ELLA** hangs up the phone, eats her lunch.)*

AGNES. How is she?

*(**ROZA** shrugs.)*

Lunch?

*(**ROZA** nods.)*

Ok.

*(**ROZA** exits.)*

*(**AGNES** puts away her things, watches **ELLA**, sits. It hits her in waves.)*

(**AGNES** *sits and stares, tension emanating.*)

(*Lights fade.*)

(*quiet*)

(*Sound of a train passing far in the distance*)

4

(Lights fade up.)

(ELLA *and* **AGNES** *are exactly where we left them.)*

(ELLA *is still eating.)*

(Several beats)

AGNES. It's quiet.
It's too quiet here. It feels like a waiting room.
You should open a window.

(AGNES *stands to open it)*

ELLA. Leave it

(AGNES *ignores her and opens the window, leans out.*
ELLA *is surprised, this is irregular.)*

(beat)

AGNES. *(softly)* Help!

(beat)

ELLA. What?

(Beat. Nothing happens.)

AGNES. Nothing. Help me write– **(AGNES** *starts jotting)* eggs, bread, what else?

ELLA. bananas, and not green ones this time either, the last batch never ripened

AGNES. bananas…

ELLA. I want some ice cream, with real sugar, and yes I can tell the difference–

(As **ELLA** *continues to speak without sound,* **AGNES** *hears the subway announcer through the open window.)*

ANNOUNCER VO. This is the blue line, eastbound–
Next stop, see us raise the Big Top, please stand back from the doors ladies and gentlemen, they'll open soon enough!
This is the blue line, eastbound

ELLA. Are you listening?

AGNES. What? Yes.

ELLA. And I don't like that new tea, so get my usual, and I guess that Darjeeling will go to waste, or you can drink it since you're so hell bent on trying new things, but don't expect me to.

AGNES. Ok, got it.

I'll go end of shift, yah?

ELLA. Hm

*(**AGNES** exits.)*

*(A bird chirps, **ELLA** looks up and out. Beat. She resumes eating.)*

(sound of subway train in the distance)

(Lights fade.)

5

(In the dark, sound builds into a loud subway symphony, culminating in sound of subway doors opening, as lights reveal **SHIPKOV***, the train driver.)*

*(***BUSKER*** plays on the platform.)*

*(***SHIPKOV*** talks at the passengers on the platform through the glass, makes up little voices for them. This is for his own enjoyment, they can not hear him.)*

SHIPKOV. Step right up, step right up!

Come on, get on, what are you looking at?

Idiot.

"oh, my nail, I broke it, what will the other girls think..."

"I am looking very handsome today, and it is clear that everyone is noticing me, oh wait, that one hasn't seen me yet, maybe I'll knock the old lady down with my immensely muscular shoulders and impress her..."

"I wonder if this is the right train, it's so confusing, oh no, another map, must not look at it as it will only confuse me more, I will just stare at the train and feel if it's the right train, because my feelings are important and valuable..."

Come on, come on, wake up!

Fuuuuuck!

BUSKER/ANNOUNCER V/O. Please stand back from the doors, this is the Blue line westbound, please stand clear of the doors.

*(***HAPPY*** rushes to* **SHIPKOV***'s door and starts to get in.* **SHIPKOV** *blocks him.)*

SHIPKOV. Hey!

HAPPY. Sorry, man, sorry

SHIPKOV. Who the fuck are you?

HAPPY. I– I'm Happy

SHIPKOV. And I am fucking pissed, get off my train

HAPPY. I'm Happy, we met yesterday, right?

You're training me.

You're training me, we met yesterday!

(long loaded beat)

(SHIPKOV *laughs loudly.)*

SHIPKOV. I'm just fucking you, get the fuck in, let's go!

HAPPY. Shit! Oh God. Ok!

(SHIPKOV *is still laughing as the doors shut, platform noise and Busker out.)*

(Sound of train driving into the tunnel, lights and sound change. Isolation on **SHIPKOV** *and* **HAPPY.)**

SHIPKOV. Should have seen your face!

Happy! Happy! What kind of stupid ass name is that anyway?

HAPPY. You asked me that yesterday.

It is a nickname, not my real name... my mother said I was a very happy baby–

SHIPKOV. Yeah yeah whatever, right?

HAPPY. Yeah. Right...

SHIPKOV. When I was a baby I climb out from my – what is it – crib and crawl outside on the steps where my mother leave this electric hotplate to cool, and I put my hand on it like this and it burn me right? So I go Waaah! pick up one hand, put the other hand on it Waaah! and I go like that Waaah! Waaah! *(miming alternating hands on the hotplate)* Waaah! until they come and lift me up. My mother say 'not so smart, but he can climb!'

HAPPY. That's a great story

SHIPKOV. Fuck you

You tell your mother she should have name you something good, like Rich. Richie Rich.

HAPPY. Ok

SHIPKOV. I got lots of great stories. You don't piss me off maybe I tell you more. Maybe teach you something, you can be all grown up. Maybe you grow up from an adjective to a, what you want to be, a noun? A proper noun? Haha! Hear that? I gotta call my ESL teacher tell her I use that shit in a sentence

Ok, you drive–

HAPPY. Really?

SHIPKOV. Don't be an asshole, no not really, the computer is fucking driving. You practice just standing there

HAPPY. ok, man!

(**HAPPY** *stands.* **SHIPKOV** *watches him, finds him comical.*)

(*beat*)

(*The dispatcher's voice comes through the radio.*)

BUSKER/DISPATCHER VO. Shipkov, come in

SHIPKOV. I am in, out

BUSKER/DISPATCHER VO. Yeah, ok, can you take third shift Friday? Collie's got a wedding or something, out

SHIPKOV. And I have nothing, no reason to be above ground, third shift Friday is ok

BUSKER/DISPATCHER VO. Uh. Ok, I'll put you down then.

SHIPKOV. Put me down as much as you want my friend

(*beat*)

BUSKER/DISPATCHER VO. over and out

SHIPKOV. It's never over and you're never out.
Idiot.
You start pushing the brake now–

BUSKER/ANNOUNCER VO. (*muted*) Please stand clear of the doors, the train is approaching the station. Please stand clear of the doors.

(*Train is pulling into the station.* **SHIPKOV** *looks out at the platform.*)

SHIPKOV. Hah. You like looking at people?

HAPPY. Sure

SHIPKOV. So look now. That's what they look like when they are in the 'off' position.

That's what people look like with no audience, no show I'd help them out, but I'm not in that business any more.

Fucking cows. Mooooo

HAPPY. Cows are holy, man

(Train stops.)

SHIPKOV. We on break now, come back in an hour.

(beat)

Open the fucking doors.

(Subway doors open, lights shift.)

6

(Ella's apartment)

(Distant sounds of the outside world are invading her quiet through the window that **AGNES** *left open)*

*(***ELLA*** *is on the phone leaving a message.)*

ELLA. Frederick, I'm extremely frustrated. I expect these women to adhere to my wishes, I expect to be in control of my own environment, but you know how these people can, well anyway call me back, I really don't know where you are, well you know where I am and I'm not going anywhere, so you could stop by, that would be appreciated. Well...

The steady mechanical hum of your absence is very soothing.

I can't sleep with all this noise.

Ok. Bye, bye.

*(***ELLA*** *hangs up, stares at the open window.)*

At least it's not winter or I'd probably catch pneumonia. Probably what she wants.

(Birds chirp.)

Birds. Stay out, stay out...

They're probably nesting on the side of the building, I should call pest control.

Anyone could get in

(Lights shift.)

7

(Roza and Shipkov's apartment)

*(**ROZA** feeds the birds at the window)*

ROZA. Heeey, pile pile pile–   *(Heeey, bird bird bird–*
kak e dumata…   *what's the word…)*

Bird… bird!

Heeeeeey bird bird bird.

Moment, chakai malko…   *(Hold on, one moment)*

Eto… hapni de, hapni–   *(There… eat, come on*
                          eat–)

Kakvo pravish tuka? Ah?   *(What are you doing*
                            here?)

Ela po blisko…   *(Come closer…)*

Haide…   *(Come on…)*
*(**ROZA** beckons the bird*
closer)
Ela, ela…   *(Come, come…)*

*(**SHIPKOV** enters from elsewhere in the apartment, pulling his pants up. **ROZA** ignores him.)*

SHIPKOV. You're home.

What the hell are you doing?

You feeding the fucking birds again?

I'm going back to work now, why don't you stay here and feed birds.

No really don't move.

*(**ROZA** does not respond. It's as though he does not exist.)*

Your ass is getting fatter every day. I notice this because it's always pointed at me. Me and your ass we have long conversations, 'hey, how you doing?'

(fart noise)

'oh really? well, my day sucked'

(fart noise)

'ok then see you later'

(**SHIPKOV** *makes fart noises all the way out, exits.*)

(**ROZA** *stands very still.*)

(*Lights shift.*)

8

(**AGNES**'s apartment)

(**AGNES** is on the phone.)

AGNES. Hello Eugene? What you doing home, what time is it over there?

– Oh, right… hey, is Granny there?

– No, I just needed to talk to your Granny…

– Oh, well, anyway… how is school?

– You need to concentrate, Eugene, those other boys can goof around but you are my smart boy, you can be president!

– Well, I think an honorable president would be better, don't you? The other kind gets killed off in very bloody manners.

– Sure you still get killed off, but it seems to me it's less bloody.

– Of course that makes a difference, you are going to die anyway, so how you do it makes a difference.

– Eugene, Eugene this is a morbid conversation, I don't care what you do, be a shopkeeper if that suits you better, your life expectancy there should be fine. Do you talk like this in school? It is a wonder your teachers don't spank you!

– Well Mr. Roberts should be careful what he tells impressionable young boys, Social Studies sounds a bit too exciting for my taste, you should study biology. You can be a doctor! You want to be a doctor Eugene? Discover new medicines?

– Who talks like that? You better shape up boy, get through this unpleasant phase quickly before you get left behind by all the smarter kids. I'm going to tell your Granny to wash your mouth out with soap.

– Sure I can, I am in the most powerful country in the world, I can do anything. Hahaaaa! Black ops with soap in their holsters, on their way right now, stand back from the door my boy, they are coming for you! No you're lying! No you!

– Ok, enough of this goofin' around, I don't got time for stories! You concentrate on your studies, hear?

– And listen to your Granny, turn out she right about every damn thing. So you pay attention, and keep your feet on the ground, don't let me hear otherwise.

– Just press your cheek.

– Do it you lazy boy!

(She kisses the phone.)

You feel that baby?

– Good. That's how much I love you.

– Nothing important, nothing really, tell granny I'll call later.

(AGNES *hangs up abruptly.)*

Shit…

(She walks to the window. Birds–)

Don't get so damn excited, I ain't birdfood yet.

(Lights shift.)

9

(**HAPPY** and **SHIPKOV** are driving.)

ANNOUNCER VO. This is the Blue line, Eastbound. This is the Blue line, Eastbound.

(beat)

HAPPY. Hey, do you ever get to announce?

SHIPKOV. What?

HAPPY. To announce. Announce the stations, man.

SHIPKOV. It's fucking automated

HAPPY. Yeah but it would be fun to do, right? I could do a great job!

SHIPKOV. Yeah, sure

HAPPY. I have a great voice

SHIPKOV. So, is that how you getting rich? You gonna to be a rockstar? 'He started as a subway announcer, and one day mr. bigshot record producer was on the train because his Porsche was in the shop, and he said that's the voice I've been looking for!'

HAPPY. That's how it happens, man!

Ok, I'm just joking about that, but my voice is going to be my fortune, that part is true. I have many business deals going on, many deals. You just got to be in the right place at the right time! That's my specialty. Hey, you want to be my partner? Fifty/fifty! I give you the easy job, I do all the work. We get rich together, ok old man?

SHIPKOV. Hey, here's a riddle! What's 50% of shit?

More shit!

HAPPY. Ok, you are not very much an optimist. Here you live in greatest country in the world and you are very negative.

SHIPKOV. Optimists are stupid people.

Do you know how depressing my damn life is?

HAPPY. Maybe you need a nickname

SHIPKOV. What?

HAPPY. My life is very 'Happy'!

SHIPKOV. Oh, haha

HAPPY. It's really too bad your mother named you 'Pissed off dude living underground in the dark'

SHIPKOV. You watch yourself

That's very fucking funny.

Asshole.

HAPPY. I think you are jealous of my name

SHIPKOV. Ha

HAPPY. Haha!

But I'm not joking man, my name keeps me safe from bad thoughts! Do you know I have had four jobs this year already? My last boss was a very unstable person, mentally you know! A different person would be very depressed, but not me man! Good thing I have a positive outlook, right?

SHIPKOV. You are proof that god has a sense of fucking humor.

HAPPY. Oh, ok, when I am famous I will still say 'hello' to you, man. That is the sort of person I am.

SHIPKOV. Famous! Ok, I'll tell you something. You ever watch a trapeze artist? Hell, you ever been to the circus?

HAPPY. Sure.

I have! I have been to the circus, I'm Indian!

SHIPKOV. Right, with a bunch of elephants sitting and standing, or did you have artists? Real artists – acrobats, trapeze/

HAPPY. India has great circus, man/

SHIPKOV. Ok, you ever look at the face of a trapeze artist? They keep their eyes open, they do what they need to do, they move forward, next act, keep moving, audience gets bored. You can't do that, you can't keep your eyes open, then I don't know, maybe you should go sell shoes or some shit, you need to think about that.

And the trap's not the big brass fucking ring, it's the next step, it's get to the other side, just moving through space, just staying alive!

There. That was a fucking metaphor, if you can't figure it out tough shit for you.

HAPPY. You really like the circus.

SHIPKOV. Yeah, whatever. I used to be Ringmaster. Another life.

Circus is like life. Only better.

HAPPY. Ok, so Ringmaster, what's your big plan?

SHIPKOV. Fuck you talking about?

ANNOUNCER VO. *(muted)* This is the Blue line, Eastbound. This is the Blue line, Eastbound.

HAPPY. What's your big plan, man? Life plan, you know.

SHIPKOV. Ok, so the metaphor, whshoo, right over your head, ok, not too bright, now I know and I won't waste my time

This, this right here, my friend, this is my plan.

I plan to stand right here, pushing this lever, for the rest of my fucking life

HAPPY. This is your dream?

SHIPKOV. No fuckhead, this is my life. Dreams are for morons, dreams are the trap, whatever, shut up, I'm finished talking to you

HAPPY. You have a very depressing outlook, I think. Not me, man, I got to think positive! I mean, no offense, but I won't be here very long, you know?

ANNOUNCER V/O. *(muted)* The train is approaching the station, please stand back from the doors, change trains to the Red line or Green line. The train is approaching the station.

SHIPKOV. *(overlaps)* Ok, watch this, let's see if anyone gets killed today– oppa! My money's on that guy with the briefcase, watch, he'll lean forward to pick it up, will he make it back up before I snap his head off?

HAPPY. Shit man

SHIPKOV. Ohhhhaaaa! Bravo! Da! By a millisecond he survives to go to work and live another boring ass day. What? This is great stuff!

(The sound of train stopping, subway doors open, lights shift.)

10

(The subway platform)

(BUSKER *plays.)*

(AGNES *is having an imaginary conversation with Eugene.)*

AGNES. So Eugene, your ma's a big fat liar, I ain't coming back.

Why? Oh, I finally heard back from the CIA and they need me to go deep undercover.

For life.

(She drops the imaginary conversation.)

Yeah there I go again, that's a damn tall tale, can't seem to help myself, which is how I ended up in this damn place. Stupid.

Yes ma, you were right about everything, Agnes thought she was special, Agnes thought she could fly, Agnes should have stayed put, stayed in her place, then maybe Agnes wouldn't be standing on this damn platform waiting for a damn train to go to the damn grocery store–

I'm bloody dying, let me go pick up some groceries.

Hey, I should get some new shoes for winter

No wait, I won't be around for winter!

Well that's a time saver!

What I need is some travel size shampoo and conditioner, little tiny bottles, that should last me!

Bullshit

This is bullshit

This is not me. This is some other woman whose life got screwed up. Not me.

No way I'm bloody dying before my own bloody punch line.

(ROZA *enters platform, stands on the edge. This is a game she plays with herself, the count down to jumping in front of the train. But she does not jump.)*

\ve, edno... op   *(Three, two, one... op)*

?

(sound of a train passing and departing)

Hey, sorry! That's the express. It don't stop here.

I only mention it cuz you looked like you was gon' hop on whether it stopped or no

Yeah, ok, good talk

You and me, we never really connected what with the language barrier. Tell truth, I don't much care, no offense, but you not that pleasant.

Well this is nice.

Guess what? I got cancer!

Eating away at my insides. Next stop, Dead Liberian woman laying on the platform! Please stand back from the damn doors, or she'll take you down with her!

Well, it's good to get that off my chest!

Thanks for listening, you blank faced cipher, boy there's nothing back there, is there?

This is great, life's full of these precious moments, right here. I got a whole series of them, lining up like empty frames going back bloody years

(They both stare ahead, long moment.)

Roza, Roza, Roza... now would be a really shitty time for you to suddenly start talking English, you wouldn't do that to me, would you?

(sound of train arriving)

No. That's my girl. Consistent, and I appreciate that.

*(**ROZA** burps and sways.)*

Hey...

Roza...?

Well, shit girl!

Are you drunk?

(Subway doors open, lights shift.)

11

(**ELLA**'s *apartment*)

(*The birds are getting louder.*)

(**ELLA** *addresses them.*)

ELLA. What?

What, are you having some sort of meeting? What are you all staring at?

Move along.

What the hell is going on, it's like a damn invasion!

(*She dials the phone, waits.*)

Frederick, they're flocking, the noise is getting out of hand.

Are you aware that starlings are highly invasive? I wouldn't put it past them to move in here and nest on my head, and the crazy Hungarian woman would probably just cluck around and feed them my lunch! I'm all alone here... it would be nice if you called to check in once in a while.

And I'll tell you this, the penthouse is not all it's cracked up to be, all I've got to look at all day is birds, it's like being condemned to the damn nature channel 24/7! And I'm the petrified wood! With no human contact but the mute and the African! Am I piquing your interest? Come see the freakshow!

(*She hangs up, watches the assembling birds.*)

I'm peeing. I'm peeing, where is everybody? I'm not supposed to sit in it.

(*Subway doors shut, lights shift.*)

12

(**SHIPKOV** *on break in his train car, coffee in hand.*)

(**ROZA** *and* **AGNES** *appear at his door.*)

(*He sees them and jumps, spills.*)

ROZA. *(to* **SHIPKOV***)* Ubiets!   *(Killer! You killed me!)*
Ti me ubi

SHIPKOV. Ah! What the   **AGNES.** Oh Shit!
fuck

Ah! What the fuck   Oh Shit!
You? I killed you?   Sorry man, sorry!
What the fuck did I   We shouldn't be here,
ever do to you except   we'll get out of your
exactly what you   way...
wanted.
Huh?   Roza! Hey come on–

(**ROZA** *ignores both of them, stumbles and sits in the
back, passes out.*)

(to **AGNES***)* What the   **AGNES.** We just got lost, she's
fuck?   not herself...

(**ROZA** *snores*)

AGNES. Hey, Roza...   **SHIPKOV.** What the fuck you
                               do to my wife?

AGNES. Your what?

SHIPKOV. My fucking passed out drunk wife over there

AGNES. I... I'm sorry, man... I just offered to take her
home, and she brought me here

SHIPKOV. Fucking bullshit.

You're not supposed to be in here, I only got five more
minutes break time

AGNES. Ok, sorry

SHIPKOV. You the black one

(*beat*)

AGNES. Yes

SHIPKOV. Yeah.

Well welcome to my humble cave, can I offer you a drink?

(He pulls out a flask.)

AGNES. No, that's–

You drink and drive?

SHIPKOV. Never! Can't. If some idiot gets killed they test you for alcohol, like it would matter, so I'm always stone cold sober when I kill.

AGNES. What you talking about? Who you killed?

SHIPKOV. Many people!

Ok two people.

Jumpers, I do them a favor, understand. They stand there, "Please Shipkov! Help me end it!" And I say, ok, splat!

AGNES. You lying

SHIPKOV. Fuck no! I swear, most drivers never have a jumper their whole career, I have three already. If you count the dog.

You want or no?

*(**AGNES** hesitates for a moment, takes the flask and sips.)*

Sit the fuck down, don't stand there drinking like some fucking hobo, you sit and drink like a civilized person. A little conversation, a little relaxation, that is the way to drink. I'll tell you to fuck off when you gotta go.

AGNES. Thanks, I wouldn't want to intrude

SHIPKOV. Yeah

*(**ROZA** snores.)*

Look at her snoring like an old woman… what the fuck you do to her, huh?

That woman used to be able to drink anybody under the fucking table, this fucking country!

AGNES. If this is what she drinking, it's small wonder she out cold

SHIPKOV. Mother's milk, you keep practicing, you'll get the hang of it. *(to* **ROZA***)* Roza, you've lost the hang of it!

(no response)

Nothing.

You know, she was the most beautiful girl in Kazanlak? I had to work hard to get her to marry me. First time I see her she is standing in a field of roses, you know Bulgarian roses? They are very famous, most beautiful, the smell is powerful, like a drug. I am visiting my uncle in Kazanlak, it's located in the valley of the roses, and I take a walk and she is standing there, cutting or some shit, and she looks up and I say, that's my woman! I tell my cousin, I will marry that one! He laughs, she says no to everyone he says, all the men in town have tried.

AGNES. Really? So how did you do it?

SHIPKOV. Eh, she like me, it was no problem. She wanted to travel, you know? I was circus man, Ringmaster, very powerful, very glamorous, and we travel all over Bulgaria. So. *(to* **ROZA***)* And you see what happens woman? We could have stayed home for this bullshit! I could have worked at the Kalashnikov factory for this bullshit!

AGNES. What, like the– *(She mimes machine gun fire.)*

SHIPKOV. Yeah. All our relatives worked there. That one? *(He points to* **ROZA***.)* She could put together a rifle in thirty–three seconds, ra–ta–ta!
Me? Thirty–eight every time.

AGNES. Roza.

SHIPKOV. Mm. But can't kill a fly. Except with her tongue. A tongue like a razor, that one!

AGNES. Yeah. And she miss chatty chatty, I don't know how you shut her up

SHIPKOV. Hey, she talk plenty when I married her!

AGNES. Yeah? What did you do to her?

SHIPKOV. Shit all nothing, we come here, the woman go crazy, turn into some sort of mute, only talk to birds anymore, walk around the subway like some fucking cow–

–You're a fucking cow! Mooing around, fucking ugly as shit!

(**ROZA** *snores.*)

AGNES. I don't think she listening

SHIPKOV. Who gives a fuck

I tell you something, the most beautiful women in the world are Bulgarian. You know why? Because for centuries, English, French, Italian, Tartar, Turk, hell every fucking army you can think of, marched through us on the way to something more important, and you know what they did? They drank, fucked, pillaged, moved on. We have dark women, light women, every kind, beautiful girls with dark skin and blue eyes, light hair, black eyes, gypsies, all mixed up. Fucking beautiful women.

AGNES. Sounds great, why did you move here?

SHIPKOV. Won the fucking lottery

(**AGNES** *starts laughing.*)

You think that's a joke? It's funny like death is funny. We won the damn green card lottery!

(**AGNES** *laughs harder.*)

You crazy, woman. They all crazy where you come from?

AGNES. I don't remember

SHIPKOV. You not American, you got an accent like me

AGNES. It's not a damn accent, it's a dialect man! I'm Liberian.

SHIPKOV. Same difference

AGNES. It's not the same bloody difference. My first language is English, your first language is Russian or something

SHIPKOV. Fucking Bulgarian

AGNES. Oh sure, like that's a real language

(*He stares, then laughs.*)

SHIPKOV. Black people are very funny

AGNES. Oh shit!

SHIPKOV. Haaaa Ha Ha Ha!

AGNES. You need to shut your mouth!

SHIPKOV. Can't! I got the gift! The gift of gabbary

AGNES. Of the gab?

SHIPKOV. Of talking

AGNES. The gift of the gab

SHIPKOV. No, the gift of talking, what the fuck? You making up words now? In your 'dialect'?

AGNES. You were trying to say the gift of gab, but you said something else/

SHIPKOV. I just said gift/

AGNES. Like in Hungarian or whatever/

SHIPKOV. Gift horse/

AGNES. What? Shut up!

SHIPKOV. My mouth is like a horse carrying a gift/

AGNES. Stop! Stop talking, man!

(*beat*)

SHIPKOV. That's what I'm telling you, I got to gab–!

(*She is bent over laughing, he watches her, laughing too.* **AGNES** *starts coughing.*)

(*Then subway silence*)

AGNES. So… a ringmaster, what exactly is that? Did you have an act, or did you just talk a lot?

SHIPKOV. Hey hey hey hey hey I talk great! That is a Ringmaster's job, my talk is like high wire act, one wrong word and it is all over, the crowd turns on you, the animals go crazy, the Big Top falls down on your head…!

AGNES. Mm

SHIPKOV. See? No one appreciates!

Ok, I did have one bit, great bit– s(
peze group come into ring, they all c
I introduce, oppa!, they swing, so on
The last one climbs up the ladder and I look at him
and say 'what's wrong with you?'

(puts on voice) 'I'm sorry boss, I can't, I'm too scared!'

'You have to!'

'I can't!'

'You have to!'

'I can't! I want to come down!' Then I take the ladder
away, fwoop! 'Boss, boss, what are you doing?'

'No one told you to climb up there! You climbed up
there, the only way out now is to fly!'

Everyone is clapping for him to jump on the trap to
the other side, I say 'the nice people paid good money,
now go! 3, 2, 1…' and he does a few more 'oh no, oh
no,' and then "OP!" he jumps!

Everyone is cheering. Great bit.

That's what they come to the circus for, you know? It's
mythos. To see a man leap like that, it's… The crowd
goes *(long inhale)* ahhhhhhh! That. That is the sound
of the soul.

ANNOUNCER VO. *(muted)* This is the Blue line, eastbound,
please stand back from the doors, the train will depart
shortly.

SHIPKOV. Yeah, you got to fuck off now.

AGNES. Yeah, thanks for the drink

SHIPKOV. Na zdrave. To your health, you know.

(beat)

AGNES. You too.

*(**SHIPKOV** looks back at **ROZA**.)*

KOV. Shit. What the fuck am I supposed to do with her?

(**AGNES** *gathers her things, glances at* **ROZA**)

AGNES. Take her for a ride

ANNOUNCER VO. Next stop Sofia Station, please stand back from the doors! Next stop Sofia Station

(**AGNES** *exits*)

(*Lights flicker, then isolate on* **ROZA**, *sleeping on the train. There is the sound of overground train departing.*)

(**BUSKER** *enters car and looks at* **ROZA**.)

(*He pulls a horn from his coat and honks, she jumps, wakes. This is young* **ROZA**, *before leaving Bulgaria. The* **BUSKER** *is* **BOBO** *the clown.*)

ROZA.Kakvo po dyavolite, ya si–	(*What the hell, get your–*)

(*she sees Bobo*)

Bobo! Kakvo pravish tuka be?	(*Bobo! What are you doing here?*)

SHIPKOV. What the hell is going on back there?

(**SHIPKOV** *enters train compartment, and is immediately in the past.*)

Bobo! Boboli, Bobentse, Bobo Booboo!

(**BUSKER/BOBO** *bows elegantly, trips and falls.* **ROZA** *rolls her eyes–*)

ROZA. Sladur, kazhi mu che tsirka e zatvoren ot edna godina!	(*Darling, tell him the circus closed a year ago!*)

SHIPKOV. (*joking*) He didn't get the official notice? The circus is closed, my man. They killed it.

(**BUSKER/BOBO** *looks at* **ROZA** *perplexed, 'what's up with the English')*

ROZA. Toi sega samo na angliiski govori
Trenira za Amerika

(He only speaks English now)
(Practicing, for America)

SHIPKOV. *(overlap)* Only English now! Training for America!

(Busker/Bobo nods sagely)

ROZA. Napravo me kefi   *(Turns me on)*

*(**SHIPKOV** laughs and grabs her ass.)*

SHIPKOV. What are you doing here, man? You got business in Sofia? New job?

*(**BUSKER/BOBO** shrugs no, looks despondent.)*

Sit, sit, have a drink!

*(**SHIPKOV** passes his flask around.)*

Now this is just like the good old days, right? The three of us after a great show, a bit of a drink to take down the adrenaline so we can get some sleep– to the best traveling circus in Bulgaria, may she rest in peace!

(They raise glasses, and toast– 'na zdrave', **BOBO** *mimes it.)*

So–!

ROZA. Bobo, mozhe bi e vreme da pochnesh da govorish otnovo

(Bobo, maybe you should start talking again)

*(**BUSKER/BOBO** gasps)*

SHIPKOV. Ey, ey, ey, Bobo, talk?! Roza! You are very insensitive woman

ROZA. Tova kvo e? Obidno li e?

(What is that? It is insulting, right?)

SHIPKOV. Bezchustvena   *(Insensitive)*

*(**ROZA** swats at* **SHIPKOV**, *he dodges, laughing.)*

ROZA. Kak mozha da go kazhesh? Ako obichash nyakoi mu kazvash istinata!   *(How can you say that? If you love someone, you tell him the truth!)*

SHIPKOV. *(overlapping and mimicking)* 'if you love someone, you tell him the truth!' You and your truth! This telling the truth is your cruelest side, woman!

The man is still in mourning, let him weep.

ROZA. Ako pochne da govori otnovo mozhe da si nameri druga rabota.   *(If he starts talking, maybe he can find another job.)*

(SHIPKOV *plants himself in front of Bobo to shield him from* **ROZA.)**

SHIPKOV. Silence is Bobo's signature! You want to take away his signature?

ROZA. Tova mu e "podpisa" kato clown!

Toi ne e veche clown!   *(It's his signature as a clown!*

He is no longer a clown!)

SHIPKOV. Once a clown, always a clown! His art is in his heart! That is what you never understand!

ROZA. Razbiram, be! No/

(BUSKER/BOBO *stops them with his horn.)*

(BOBO *places his hat on his heart, opens his mouth–)*
(Tries.

Tries.

Tries.)

(No sound comes out.)

SHIPKOV. There, you see? He's not ready.

ROZA. Dobre, dobre Bobo, ti opita.   *(Ok. Ok, Bobo, you tried.)*

Ama kato stignem do grada, tryabva da si malko po osvoboden. Te v Sofia obichat hora deto govoryat.

(But when we get to the city you need to be more flexible. In Sofia they like people who talk.)

(SHIPKOV flings his arm around BOBO.)

SHIPKOV. Please, woman! The city doesn't know what she likes!

You'll show them, right Bobo? Maybe a little more shut–up is what they need in the city.

Bobo will seduce her with his art, show her what's good for her... women always fall for the man who makes them laugh

ROZA. Mmm, tova li mi se sluchi na men?

(Oh, is that what happened to me?)

(BOBO pulls ROZA to her feet, dances with her, romances her. SHIPKOV watches her dance with open enjoyment.)

SHIPKOV. You didn't stand a chance woman

ROZA. Umnata zhena vinagi pozvolyava na mazha da si vyarva.

(A smart woman always lets a man believe that.)

(BOBO twirls her.)

Oh Bobo!   *(Oh, Bobo!)*

SHIPKOV. Ok, ok, ok, that's enough! Get your own!

(SHIPKOV grabs ROZA's hand. BOBO releases ROZA tragically. She twirls and lands on SHIPKOV's lap, kissing him.)

(BOBO politely looks the other way.)

Bobo, Bobo, Bobo! Me and Roza, we got lucky! We taking our act to the USA! Move over world, here we come, ah? Move your ass, or I'll go all Archimed on your ass and get a lever and do it for you! Me and Roza gonna need a whole lotta space!

ROZA. Tochno taka, sladur!   *(You got it, babe!)*

SHIPKOV. But you keep doing the work here and we'll meet again my friend…

You know what you tell them, Bobo? You tell everyone you see. People say the circus is dying, but it's not dying, it's just changing, and we have to change with it! All the artists will still have a place, we just need to find what that place is now. Things are different that is all. We move to the next town, we put together a new act, people will come and watch, you'll see! You tell people that.

You are an artist, Bobo. You are a star. That is all!

(BUSKER/BOBO *winks at* ROZA *and mimes 'drunk'.)*

(ROZA *nods, laughs.*)

SHIPKOV. Shut up, man!

(*sound of train arriving*)

ROZA. Na dobar chas, Bobo,   (*Best of luck, Bobo*
Boboli, Bobentse.   *Boboli Bobentse*)

(ROZA *kisses* BUSKER/BOBO *on the lips.*)

(*Lights flicker, we are back in the present,* BOBO *is gone.* ROZA *facing away from* SHIPKOV.)

SHIPKOV. Hey! You hear me?

I said, can you walk or do I have to carry your drunk ass?

(*Subway doors open, lights shift.*)

13

(Ella's apartment, she leaves a message.)

*(**AGNES** changes her diaper.)*

ELLA. Well Frederick, despite your failure to respond, I continue to keep you informed as per your request for updates on my condition, and I can inform you that my condition, diagnostically speaking, remains the same. The same cannot be said for my surroundings, the condition of my surroundings is rapidly deteriorating, as is my peace of mind, in case you were wondering which I'm sure you weren't!

Well then, what a nice chat this is, it's nice to check in once in a while, let's do this again soon. It's a good thing I'm an independent and capable individual, isn't it? Lucky you!

Ok bye bye then.

*(**AGNES** exits.)*

Shut the window before you leave!
Shut the damn–!
Shit!

(Bird chirps.)

Oh shut up! Who asked you?

(Lights shift.)

14

(Happy's apartment, **HAPPY** *is on the phone.)*

HAPPY. Hey, Pita–ji, this is your eldest son calling!

–So good, Pita–ji, so good!

–ji

–ji

–Yeah, you know how business is, it has its ups and downs, but you know me, mostly ups, right?

–Well, there is this investment opportunity, I am thinking very hard, may be big, very big... the investment is a little bigger than I can...

–Achah, yeah...

–So what I was saying is the investment is a little bigger that I can afford right now, I don't know, I'm thinking about it...

–Thinking about if I can afford to do it, you know. But when an opportunity is this big, can I afford to not do it, you know?

–Well yeah, it's just a cash flow problem. Sometimes the checks some at the wrong time to seize the opportunity, all of a sudden I'll have all the money I need but two days too late, you know how it is.

Maybe you have some money you can send, just for a week, and I can–?

–No, of course not, ji.

–No, I don't really need it, I was mostly thinking to do you a favor, it is a very good opportunity, but no, don't send money, I need nothing, I have everything I need pita–ji!

–Okay ji. Give my love to Ma, ok?

–Ok.

*(**HAPPY** hangs up, lights shift)*

15

(Ella's apartment)

*(**ELLA** sleeps.)*

*(**AGNES** sits on the floor in the dark, kind of drunk. She is having an imaginary conversation with Eugene.)*

AGNES. So, Eugene, how you doing! I called to say I met this ringmaster, and I been invited to join the circus. Turns out I'm a natural! So I'll be taking off soon then, on that there circus train, so I guess we won't be talking on the phone no more...

Cuz there's no signal...

On the train...

It's an underground circus.

*(**AGNES** is laughing. **ROZA** enters, rushed.)*

Hey, you back!

Don't worry, I covered for you.

Come on in, pull up some floor.

(birds)

Have you ever heard him call her back? Her son... Frederick... Freddie...?

She just leaves messages upon messages, and they ain't short neither, can you imagine coming home and there's a bloody novel on your answering machine. I bet he don't even listen to them! It's sad really, I should feel pity

*(**AGNES** makes up a story.)*

The wooden queen had a son, a handsome prince, whom she bore in absentia, having deposited her womb with a top-rated OB/GYN to be on the safe side. She checked in on the phone daily, but one day while she was out, he was born. From his navel stretched an umbilical telephone cord. Without fully considering the potential consequences, the doctors cut that cord, separating mother from son.

AGNES. *(cont.)* She still checks in daily, but he hasn't answered the phone since.

(**AGNES** *laughs.*)

(**ROZA** *starts laughing.*)

AGNES. *(cont.)* Whatchu laughing at?

Roza…

Oh shit. You bitch!

You understood that.

You understood that.

Oh man, you are so busted! I'm gon' have to tell Ella now!

(**ROZA** *grabs* **AGNES,** *wrestles her down, covering her mouth. They're both laughing.*)

No no, get away from me! You can't stop me from doing the right thing! Ella! Ella!

(**ELLA** *stirs in her sleep.*)

ELLA. Damn birds

(**AGNES** *and* **ROZA** *laugh even harder, muffled behind their hands.*)

AGNES. Sh! Roza, shut it, you talk too much!

Man!

(**AGNES** *starts coughing, after a while they settle down.*)

(birds)

(to the bird) What you looking at? Look like my granny, same beady eyes…

I screwed up. With my stories and my bullshit. I screwed up, thought I knew shit, but I didn't.

Agnes thought she knew shit and then she died, the end.

All my granny's fault, she filled my head with tall tales, crazy stories, 'the taller the better' she used to say, 'I like the view from up there!' My ma would get so mad, 'don't you go filling that girl's head with that nonsense!'

And then I went and did the same thing to my boy, telling him stories... I stopped though, I learned my damn lesson. So why I got to be punished? I stopped telling stories, no matter how hard he begs, I don't tell them no more, I been humbled, so why I got to be punished now huh?

The higher they climb, the harder they fall, right?

Yeah.

I tell you this though, my umbilical telephone cord is fully intact man. Me and my boy we talk all the time, he know I'm part of his life!

He got to grow up, focus on what's real, right...?

He won't turn out like me, no way. I always been... insufficiently tethered to reality

A loose tether

That's me

Just that one umbilical... telephone cord... that's all I got...

(Sound of birds, **AGNES** *looks out the window.)*

My boy gon' be tethered!

ROZA. Good

AGNES. A boring life ain't the end of the damn world, right?

Right?

ROZA. Yes.

No.

AGNES. Why am I asking you?

Like you got such rock solid relationships! Maybe with them birds? They talk back much?

ROZA. If you listen

AGNES. At least I got someone, what you got?

ROZA. Skorets

AGNES. Damn, I got to go.

    *(***AGNES*** exits.)*

ROZA. Skorets…

    The birds– Skorets. Starling. They talk.

    Make mimika– *(She makes bird sounds.)* piu piu piu KRA KRA piu piu piu 'hello Freddie' piu piu KRA…

    (Lights shift.)

16

(**SHIPKOV** *and* **HAPPY** *on break in the train.*)

(**HAPPY** *is restless and claustrophobic.*)

HAPPY. Hey, you ever been on top of this thing?

SHIPKOV. What?

HAPPY. Top of the train, the roof man! Come on, let's go!

SHIPKOV. What the hell you talking about? That's maintenance job.

HAPPY. No, man, on top of the train is the best way to travel– only idiots get stuck inside.

In India I travel only on the roof, all my friends, we talk, the wind is blowing, up so high you can see the world! We have to yell to hear, and crazy stories man, crazy stories! That is the life, wind blowing, flying so fast if you let go or stand up, you're dead man!

SHIPKOV. In Bulgaria they see you on top of the roof they shoot you down with Kalashnikov, ackackackackackacka

HAPPY. Why man?

SHIPKOV. Why you think? It's not safe up there, you must be saved from your stupidity. Ha!

HAPPY. That's very bad karma

SHIPKOV. Fucking karma

HAPPY. You shouldn't dismiss karma, man, it's serious shit. Karma is why you keep killing people.

SHIPKOV. What the hell you talking about, killing people?

HAPPY. It's that bad KGB karma

SHIPKOV. Yeah, except I'm not KGB, I'm fucking Bulgarian

HAPPY. Same thing

SHIPKOV. It is not the fucking same thing, I'm fucking Bulgarian!

HAPPY. Ok, you know what you do if you want to stop killing people? You tie a child's shoe to the front of the train, that will block your bad karma

SHIPKOV. That's stupid

HAPPY. It's true man, take it or leave it. Friend of mine, a truck driver from Chandigarh, did that and he never hit anybody

SHIPKOV. Astonishing

HAPPY. Ok fine, keep killing people

SHIPKOV. Ok fine–

What about your fucking karma?

HAPPY. I've got great karma! When I was born my father told me I'm going to be great. 'It is your destiny to move the world,' my father said, 'you just need to find your path.' I'm finding my path, and then, boom!

SHIPKOV. Wow. Another fucking star. You are everything that I hate.

HAPPY. Come on, man

SHIPKOV. You. You are what killed the circus. People like you. Used to be people would come to the circus to see, to feel, to sit in the audience and be scared, and cry, and laugh and live the beautiful and terrible life before going home all safe and sound. Now every Tom, Dick and Asshole thinks he should be in the damn Ring doing the tricks himself. Everyone's pushing and shoving to get in the spotlight, no one trains, no one wants to sit in the audience and see someone better than them perform, everyone has to be a damn star. It's chaos, no ringmaster, and no one cares.

HAPPY. I'm not listening to you, you're just trying to depress me

SHIPKOV. Hey, you want to move the world?

(SHIPKOV *takes the controls*).

Here's some real philosophy– Archimed said– 'Give me a place to stand and a lever long enough and I will move the world.' You ever hear that?

Look at me! I got a lever– sloow, fast, sloow, fast, stop… I'm moving the world! 'Ok people, get on, who wants to move? Great sir, I'll move you anywhere you want on the blue line!'

How about that! Isn't life great? I'm a fucking titan! I have the Power! And here I am training you because I'm so fucking generous. There's your path. Congratulations, you found it.

Fuuuuck!

I'm going to take a piss, don't touch nothing.

(SHIPKOV exits, HAPPY sits.)

ANNOUNCER VO. This is the Blue line eastbound to Mumbai, please stand clear of the doors! Blue line eastbound to Mumbai!

(Lights flicker, then isolate on HAPPY on the train holding a phone.)

(This is HAPPY months ago, in a phone center in Mumbai, city noise outside.)

(BUSKER pops through the window as BUNTY, a young Indian musician.)

BUSKER/BUNTY. Come on, work's done, superstar!

(HAPPY waves him off, keeps talking on the phone, very charming.)

HAPPY. –Mrs. Joshi, this special deal I am calling to offer you is a special–!

–Ok, I'm sorry to hear that ma'm, good bye then.

–Yes thank you, good bye.

BUSKER/BUNTY. Why are you thanking her?

(HAPPY disconnects.)

HAPPY. I am a very polite person

BUSKER/BUNTY. You think you'll meet her, in the USA, maybe you will be neighbors

HAPPY. You never know, right?

Aaahhhhhh!

Good night America, good morning Mumbai!

So, what's going on, man?

(Busker pulls out a joint, lights up, they pass it back and forth.)

BUSKER/BUNTY. I'm playing a birthday party, American Embassy! Beatles, man! Birthday boy loves the Beatles, old guy is like a Beatles-in-India tourist. I'll tell my Ravi Shankar story, they'll love it! You know my Ravi Shankar story?

HAPPY. Which one?

BUSKER/BUNTY. The Beatles one stupid!

Achah, so one of them, I think George Harrison, is saying to Pandit– ji, 'Oh you are so amazing, I have to learn to play the sitar, I have to learn right now, teach me, teach me, everything you know you genius you!' Like that, very enthusiastic.

HAPPY. Sure

BUSKER/BUNTY. And Ravi Shankar looks at him and says "The Beetle must have patience."

(Beat. Bunty plays 1st few bars of 'come together', putting on his best stoned rocker face.)

HAPPY. That's a joke?

BUSKER/BUNTY. It's funny! Americans love it! 'Haasi to Phaasi'! If I make her laugh, I got her, right?!

HAPPY. They think that's funny, maybe I should be a comedian

BUSKER/BUNTY. Great idea, except you're not funny. I'm funny.

HAPPY. You're crazy man, that is not funny!

BUSKER/BUNTY. Bet?

HAPPY. I'll bet my Gandhi quote against your stupid Beatles-joke, mine will get more laughs

BUSKER/BUNTY. You just don't get it, it's in the delivery.

HAPPY. Ok, that's it, we call someone right now, an American, and we find out! Here we go, here we go!

*(**HAPPY** searches, selects, dials.)*

BUSKER/BUNTY. You're gonna get busted, man

(sound of dialtone/ringing)

HAPPY. Uh–uh *(displays the palm of his hand, grinning)*, lucky line! You see that? You see how long that is?

(A phone rings, rings…)

BUSKER/BUNTY. No one home

*(lights up on **ELLA** answering the phone)*

HAPPY. Have some patience, man! Like your beetle

ELLA. Freddie?

HAPPY. Is this Mrs. Ella Mortimer?

ELLA. What? Yes.

HAPPY. Great, how are you today ma'm?

ELLA. I'm not interested

HAPPY. I'm sorry to hear that ma'am because what I have to say is very interesting!

I wonder, do you make international calls ma'm?

ELLA. No

HAPPY. Great! Maybe I can interest you in a joke?

ELLA. What?

HAPPY. More a funny story, really. You have my guarantee that you might find it funny

BUSKER/BUNTY. That's bullshit man! You have to sell it!

ELLA. I might find it funny?

HAPPY. Well, you have to be the judge, ma'am

BUSKER/BUNTY. You have to deliver it well!

HAPPY. May I tell you the joke ma'am? It's very short, I promise!

(beat)

ELLA. Go ahead

HAPPY. Ok, so George Harrison of the Beatles, you know the Beatles ma'am?

ELLA. Of course I know the Beatles

HAPPY. Ok, so George Harrison is in India, and he is meeting with very famous Indian sitar player Ravi Shankar, and he is saying to Ravi Shankar "I want to learn everything about the sitar, I want to learn to play like you, you are so incredible, teach me everything!" Right?

ELLA. Mm–hm.

HAPPY. And Ravi Shankar looks at George Harrison and says, "The Beetle must have patience."

(beat)

ELLA. That's it?

HAPPY. That's it. *(to Bunty)* She's not laughing.

BUSKER/BUNTY. That's because if your bullshit delivery, man!

ELLA. It's not very funny

BUSKER/BUNTY. Let me tell it!

*(**BUSKER** grabs for the phone.)*

HAPPY. Back off man, I told it well, I told it as well as you can tell a stupid joke.

Hey hey hey, seriously, ma'am? Do you think I told it well?

ELLA. I suppose you were fine

HAPPY. No, come on, I was better than fine, I had comic timing and everything, it's just a bad joke

BUSKER/BUNTY. Give me the phone!

HAPPY. Let me tell you another, it's funnier!

ELLA. I don't know if I have time

HAPPY. Just one more, very quick, I promise

ELLA. OK

BUSKER/BUNTY. You already ruined mine! This doesn't count to the bet!

HAPPY. Listen and learn man. So a journalist one time asked Mahatma Gandhi, do you know Mahatma Gandhi?

ELLA. Yes

HAPPY. A journalist says to Mahatma Gandhi, " What do you think of Western Civilization?"

ELLA. Mm–hm

HAPPY. And Mahatma Gandhi answers, "I think it would be a good idea."

(beat)

HAPPY. Well?

BUSKER/BUNTY. Ha!

ELLA. That's a little funnier

HAPPY. Then why don't you laugh?

ELLA. I have to go, I'm expecting another call.

HAPPY. I'm sorry, I know you're very busy, thank you for your time ma'am!

ELLA. That's alright

HAPPY. Oh, and if you decide to start making international calls, please don't hesitate to contact us!

ELLA. Bye.

*(***ELLA*** hangs up, lights out on Ella's apartment.* ***HAPPY*** *and Bunty howl with laughter.)*

BUSKER/BUNTY. You are going to get so fired, man!

HAPPY. No way, she liked me, she won't be complaining!

BUSKER/BUNTY. You never know with Americans, man

HAPPY. Maybe I should keep this number. Hah? I think when I come to America she will be very happy to have me as her boyfriend!

BUSKER/BUNTY. You're not going anywhere

HAPPY. What are you, Stupid? Look– Travel line, it's as long as the Lucky line! I'm already a star man, it just hasn't happened yet!

BUSKER/BUNTY. Ok, you are too stupid! You have to take the number with you now. Seriously man, just in case, backup plan in case your Lucky line runs out!

*(***BUNTY*** stuffs Ella's number in* ***HAPPY****'s pocket.)*

HAPPY. Get off me, man!

BUNTY/BUSKER. Hey, you know Birju's got a system where if you just get one credit card number you can take

everything– bank accounts, name, whatever you need!
Easy, man!

HAPPY. I'm not that guy man, you know I don't mess with
my karma

BUSKER/BUNTY. What are you stupid? Americans have
insurance, man! They get all the money back, no problem! He can get you a new name with a green card
too, man, if you weren't such a coward, you could be
in America next week!

HAPPY. Birju is an idiot,   **SHIPKOV.** *(unlit)* What are
man!   you, an idiot?

HAPPY. What?

SHIPKOV. *(unlit)* You an idiot?

> *(Lights flicker, We are back in present day subway.*
> **BUSKER/BUNTY** *is gone.* **HAPPY** *is holding his phone*
> *and Ella's number.)*

SHIPKOV. Move over! What the hell is wrong with you, you
know there's no signal down here

> **(HAPPY** *moves over,* **SHIPKOV** *takes the controls.)*

HAPPY. Hey! I was just checking, you never know right?

SHIPKOV. What the hell is that?

HAPPY. What? Oh, just a phone number.

God, I'm so fucking bored!

Come on, let's go up on the roof!

SHIPKOV. I'm not going up on no roof, it's a dark fucking
tunnel, I know that, I don't need proof!

> *(Subway doors open, lights shift.)*

17

(AGNES at the window with birds)

(ELLA on the phone)

ELLA. Well, Frederick, I'm sorry to inform you that now the African has lost her grasp of the English language also, as she can no longer receive a simple instruction to shut the damn window. Here, allow me to demonstrate:

(to AGNES)

Shut The Window!

(back to Frederick)

Nothing. This is the world in which I live.

So I'll be expecting you.

(ELLA hangs up.)

Cow.

(ELLA eats. Silence.)

AGNES. The wooden queen called and called

ELLA. What?

AGNES. But no matter how many times she called him, he never answered.

ELLA. My son is none of your business

AGNES. He never answers.

ELLA. I have asked you repeatedly to shut the window

AGNES. It's just you talking into the damn air.

ELLA. This is after all my home, and you are my employee, so one might expect you to take instruction/

AGNES. If you were any kind of mother, your kid would want to talk to you!

ELLA. I don't know how you expect to retain to retain your employment

AGNES. You sit there like you something, but you're nothing, you're nobody, you don't exist! You a figment! Don't believe me?

ELLA. The only way you might redeem yourself is if you shut the window right now

AGNES. When's the last time you talked to someone who talked back?

ELLA. This is not! A conversation!

AGNES. And in that moment she ceased to exist. The end.

(**AGNES** *exits.*)

(*silence*)

(*Telephone rings, rings...***ELLA** *picks up.*)

ELLA. Frederick?

HAPPY. Mrs. Ella Mortimer?

ELLA. What? I'm not interested.

HAPPY. I'm sorry to hear that ma'am, because what I have to say is very interesting!

I wonder, ma'am, if you remember we talked once before?

My name is Happy!

Remember George Harrison?

ELLA. Long distance

HAPPY. That's right, ma'am!

ELLA. I don't call long distance

HAPPY. Oh, now, how this is possible, ma'am? Me, I make many telephone calls, every day I am making connections with people, talking with many people...

ELLA. I don't

HAPPY. It's very simple to change service/

ELLA. I don't like change

HAPPY. Come on now, you must make some telephone calls? You tell me who do you call, ma'am, and I will find the best deal I have for you!

ELLA. I don't make calls.

HAPPY. Everyone makes calls!

ELLA. The only person I call is my son Frederick, but/

HAPPY. Ok, great, Frederick is a very nice name! And where does he live, ma'am?

ELLA. I have to go/

HAPPY. Maybe your son would like it if you saved some money on calling him! So he doesn't have to feel so guilty, and then you can talk longer together and spend less money together, it is good for everyone! You think Frederick would like that, ma'am?

ELLA. No

HAPPY. I'm sure he would, I think about these things, a son thinks about these things, trust me I know! I think Frederick would be pleased with anything that makes your life better.

ELLA. I think Frederick wouldn't care one way or another. His telephone number is disconnected.

I don't like change.

So that's alright, as not much changed with his absence.

Well, if you're still there, I'll take the long distance

HAPPY. Ma'am…

ELLA. I'll take it, I said!

HAPPY. That's ok, ma'am, if you don't need it I wouldn't feel right about selling you something you don't need, that is not good karma…

ELLA. How would you know what I need or don't need? I'll be the judge of what I need! I'll be making some calls in the future… some important…

HAPPY. Ok, you can think about it ma'am, and I can call you back at some later time that is convenient/

ELLA. It's convenient now! What sort of salesman are you? And what sort of name is Happy, anyway?

HAPPY. What?

ELLA. I said, what sort of name is Happy? It sounds ridiculous!

HAPPY. It's not my real name, it's a nickname…

My mother said I was a very happy baby…

ELLA. All babies are happy

HAPPY. Well I was extra happy! I'm just joking, it's a long story, I don't want to bore you

ELLA. I asked. Why would I ask if I wasn't interested?

HAPPY. ...on the first day after my birth, my father read my palm and said this child will travel very far. And so my mother started to cry, saying that he had destroyed her happiness. And my father said to her, "his destiny is to bring happiness to the world, when he is here he will make you happy, and when he is gone he will make other people happy, and that is how it should be. For happiness comes and goes." So they called me Happy.

ELLA. Hm

HAPPY. Yes, a nickname is a great responsibility, I take it very seriously! I'll tell you what, maybe I can interest you in a joke?

ELLA. Ha! Spare me!

(*ELLA laughs. It's rusty, but authentic.* **HAPPY** *laughs too.*)

HAPPY. Oh, ok, alright! You break my heart that you don't trust my jokes, you know?

Alright ma'am, you have a great day, I should go now

ELLA. We haven't... we haven't completed our transaction!

HAPPY. Ma'am, there is no big urgency, maybe some other time–

ELLA. Of course there is! It's now or never, that's how everything is!

Alright, now is when you take my credit card number.

It would make me Happy, alright?

HAPPY. Do you have insurance?

ELLA. You're selling insurance now? Don't get greedy, it's not appealing

HAPPY. No... I was just wondering

ELLA. Ok, let's have it!

(*Lights shift.*)

*(**AGNES** is on the platform.)*

(Imaginary conversation with Eugene)

(Sound of train approaching)

AGNES. Well hey there, Eugene.

This is Mama.

I'm dying.

I'm sorry I failed you baby.

I'm standing in the deepest darkest grotto where humankind come to wait for they date with the sleeping giant who tells they future.

There ain't no damn schedule, he just pick who he talk to when he wake up, you never know when it gon' be your turn. Once in a while you hear this rumbling roaring, and you know he stirring.

(The train is coming.)

And just before he shoot out the tunnel heading who knows where, there's this giant exhale, whoosh!

Yeah.

This damn place.

ANNOUNCER VO. Get your tickets now, this is the Blue line, eastbound to Monrovia! Get your tickets now, Blue line, eastbound to Monrovia! Please stand back from the doors.

*(Lights flicker, and isolate on **AGNES** and Busker on train.)*

*(This is young **AGNES** ten years ago in Monrovia before she left for America, sounds of street and people all around. She laughs and smokes with her friend, the **BUSKER**, who jams and listens as she talks his ear off. Her dialect is heavier, she is bright, funny, energetic.)*

AGNES. Ok look, it's no different from when Gran take care of me when Ma got that job in the city! And of course I want to be here, I want to see Eugene every day, but come on, I want him to have a real life too, right? Sissy say the money you make in America is five times, five times! So I'm askin' how can she say not go? Here's what I got planned, but do she want to stop and listen to the plan? Hell no! It's a good plan, huh? I know she scared, she scared I gon' change, get up to some foolishness, but she got to see I a grown woman now, not some small child gon' be swayed by every damn thing, I ain't gon' turn American and go off. I tell you, my slutty days are done–

Shut it! Let me talk! I know I had some parties when I came to town, but that's changed. I'm not looking for that no more, I'm not looking for Agnes no more, I found her. My real life is here with Eugene.

This thing, it's just me going to work for a while, ok for a long while, but really it's just like a day at work, right? Then I come home and we pick right up. And that's my plan, and a good one, but does ma listen? Hell no! That woman think she know everything! But it's a new world, right? She don't know this new world! You know what she tell me last night? She tell me I too young to know shit, and she wish for me a boring life. That is her greatest wish for me, a boring life! I swear I know she mean well, but the way that woman express herself, it's enough to make me mad!

You mark my words, I would never tell my kid to go have a boring life! What kind of mother says that?

(Sound of birds flying into the distance)

Hey! Look at them birds! You see that! That's me man, I'll be outta here soon!

Oh come on, don't look like that, I'll be back before you know it!

Here, pinkie oath, ah?

(They link fingers, and she laughs, loud and open.)

ANNOUNCER VO. Next stop, the US of A, please stand back from the doors. Next stop, the US of A

AGNES. Ok, I got to fly, I'll see you!

(Lights flicker, and we're back in the present day as the train is pulling to a stop.)

*(**AGNES**'s shine is gone, she is older, tired and drab. **AGNES** exits.)*

(Lights shift.)

19

(Ella's apartment, telephone rings, she answers)

ELLA. Hello?

—Oh. Yes, this is she…

—What? Yes, I made a purchase. By telephone, I made a purchase.

—Well yes of course I authorized that, that's how one makes a—

—Well that's obviously a typo, your system must be experiencing some sort of/

—Of course I haven't been there… no I didn't withdraw anything from… no I haven't gone to the… no that is not my…

—I have not gone anywhere in 30 years, dammit, I am bedridden!

(long silence)

—I have to go. I'm very busy. I'm expecting an important/

—I am not interested in your…! I know perfectly well what to do young lady, I'm not an idiot!

—No, I have no interest in reporting anything with you, you're obviously incompetent, goodbye!

(She hangs up.)

(She picks up the phone, freezes, puts it down again.)

(Lights fade.)

20

(**SHIPKOV** *on break,* **ROZA** *enters the platform.*)

ROZA. Alo! Saprugat! (*Hey! Husband!*)

SHIPKOV. Roza...?

What the hell are you doing here?

It's like you're never at home anymore, you just wander around in the subway

ROZA. Shto ne me pitash (*Why don't you ask me*
zashto? *why?*)

SHIPKOV. I know why, it's because you're crazy

So, you're talking now, huh?

Roze? What is it?

ROZA. You know why I come down here?

I... like to be close to you.

Ne moga da te gledam, (*I can't look at you, I*
ne moga da govorya c *can't talk to you, but*
teb, no vse oshte iskam *I still like to be close to*
da sam blizo do teb. *you.*)

SHIPKOV. Why? Why can't you talk to me?

ROZA. Because I am not beautiful in this country!

Ne sam! (*I'm not!*)

I sound stupid, I look stupid

Go around like a fool...

Can't tell a bloody joke!

I can't let you see me like this!

Zashtoto shte spresh (*Because you'll stop*
da me obichash *loving me*)

(**SHIPKOV** *takes it in*)

SHIPKOV. I won't stop loving you.

ROZA. But more...

You are not beautiful here

You are small. Like me.

ROZA. *(cont.)* Ti znaesh   *(You know that stupid*
tazi glupost deto vse   *thing you say about the*
raspravyash za losta na   *lever of Archimedes?)*
Arhimed?

It's bullshit.

SHIPKOV. It's all in your perspective, Roza, that's what you never understand, I am fucking Archimed! 'Give me a place to stand and a lever long enough and I will move the world!'

(ROZA *shakes her head.*)

ROZA. You have lever, but no place to stand

You move nothing

It move you

(Subway silence)

DISPATCHER VO. Shipkov, come in

SHIPKOV. Yeah, Shipkov is in

DISPATCHER VO. Just to let you know, that kid you were training, Sanjeet... uh... Joshi?

SHIPKOV. That's his fucking name?

DISPATCHER VO. Yeah, well, he took off, didn't check in today, actually there's something weird about his paperwork, could be that's not his name at all

Anyway, don't wait around for him

(silence)

You there?

SHIPKOV. Yeah.

Hell no, man, I stay on schedule

DISPATCHER VO. Ok, great, over and out

(dispatcher clicks off)

SHIPKOV. It's never over and you're never out.

Idiot.

(to ROZA*)* You want a ride home?

(She looks long at him. An understanding of sorts.)

ROZA. Ok.

(She sits in the back. He prepares to pull out of the station.)

ANNOUNCER VO. This is the Blue Line, Westbound

(Subway doors shut, lights shift.)

21

(Lights up, **ELLA** *hasn't moved.)*

(The telephone rings.)

*(***ELLA*** *does not answer, something has broken in her.)*

(The telephone rings and rings and rings.)

*(***AGNES*** *enters).*

AGNES. You want me to get that?

ELLA. No

(The telephone rings and rings.)

(The telephone finally stops ringing.)

AGNES. Ella…?

Hey, Ella!

ELLA. Do you want to hear a joke?

AGNES. What?

ELLA. One of the Beatles, George Harrison wanted to learn to play the guitar from a famous Indian musician and he begged and begged and wanted to learn it in a hurry and the famous Indian musician said 'the beetle must have patience.'

AGNES. Did you skip something?

ELLA. I don't think so

AGNES. I don't get it

ELLA. I don't get it either…

*(***ELLA*** *looks strangely vulnerable)*

AGNES. Ella?

You want me to shut the window?

Come on now, buck up woman!

Tell you what… Hey, Ella!… Tell you what…

After I go I'll come back as one of them birds and take you for a ride, ok?

You climb up on my back and see the world.

ELLA. What?

AGNES. No lie. Look at me. No lie. Just the truth stretched
out a bit. Taller. Better.

All you got to do is keep that window open for me.

What do you say, Ella?

Hm?

C'mon, here…

here…

Pinkie oath

(**AGNES** *carefully, and with difficulty, links her finger to*
ELLA*'s clawed one.*)

Like the man say

We up here now.

No way out but to fly–

(Lights shift.)

22

(Agnes's apartment)

(**AGNES** *is on the phone.*)

AGNES. Hey Eugene! Whatchu doing, baby?

–I'm great, baby, never better!

–Well, homework is boring, alright, but you got to do it. All that boring stuff is training you for the big time adventures you gon' have, right? But for now you stay on that straight path ok? Don't you worry baby, your time is coming to jump into the world. It's your calling little man. So anyway, you want a story?

–Yeah, for real!

–No it's not educational, you insult me man, don't I tell the best not-at-all-boring story in the world?

–Damn right! Alright, so the other day, there I am, minding my own business, and it happens. Outta nowhere! I got the calling: 'Agnes, you need to head out to the Terminal' the voice says. Here I am, going on with my daily routine, and Boom! Outta nowhere, '…head out to the Terminal', could have knocked me over with a feather!

–Well what do you think for? For take-off, what else? Turns out they's big things brewing, little man, there a crisis that go all the way to the top, could bring down the whole damn circus! It's time. Time for me to take my proper place!

–Ah, well, this some top secret information, I don't know if you're ready to hear it… so anyway, I just called to say good bye–

–Yeah, but you still an operative in training, don't want to tell you too much too soon… don't you worry about nothing, I'll see you later–

–Ok, if you sure. Alright, alright, but keep your voice down, some kind of secret agent you're going to make, bellowing all over the place!

–Yeah, that's better. Ok, alright... you by the window?

–No man, go to the one in the kitchen, the one over-looks the field and the telephone wires. You see any birds out there?

–That's right... they gathering... ok, now look at the sky.

Take a good look, nah?

Closer...

Closer....

You see where the fabric fraying? Some of them seams even splitting... oooo, it's a mess up there! Maintenance needs to get up there right now before the whole damn thing rips open and the Big Top comes tumbling down...

Birds gon' be busy today, keepin' it all together...

–Well, yeah the birds, what do you think they doing up there all day? They on the job! Fact, your great-granny up there, patching clouds, fixin' leaks, it's the family business, and it's time you know about it.

No lie! That's the pure truth– I'm taller, so I can see better!

Ain't everyone able to do this job, Eugene, it takes a special kind of person to leap into nothing and believe that they'll fly...

But without them people, the world just stops turning, you know?

World needs maintenance... always has, always will...

–I guess a bit of both... some fun with the flying and all, lotta work cuz that's maintenance, a job's work any way you look at it... if you ain't up for that challenge, you don't get to wear the feathers, and that's that

–Yeah, I bet you up for it... you my boy, right? It's in your blood

–Ok, now the bad news baby, I can't call once I head out, fact is we can't talk on the phone for a long time. No signal on the train.

AGNES. *(cont.)* But here's what I got planned– once I get my feathers I'm gon line up with them other birds you see out there, try to hack into a telephone wire, see if I can't call you that way, ok? You keep watching them birds, you'll see me watching you right back.

–Oh shit, there go another seam, you see that one?

–Clever boy! You got the eye!

–Ok, I got to go, baby.

–Where the Terminal? Oh, now, you know I can't tell you that!

–Ok, you'll keep it to yourself? Man, I can't believe I telling you this... ok, fine! Fine! I'm going to Darjeeling!

–Sh! Don't you go repeating it, you crazy man?? Alright. I'll see you around, yah?

–Yeah. You right. Maybe don't tell granny about the sky falling, she stressed out enough as it is.

–Press your cheek.

(She kisses the phone.)

–You feel that?

–Good. Keep them eyes open.

(AGNES hangs up.)

(She goes to the window.)

(Laughs. Coughs. Coughs. Coughs... feathers...)

BUSKER/ANNOUNCER VO. This is the Blue line that, on her first birthday in the US of A, Agnes took all the way from one end to the other to see how it began and ended, watching the telephone lines run past the window, birds lining up to get in.

When she called home that night, Agnes told Eugene his very first tall telephone tale.

AGNES. *(to birds)* Yeah, I'm coming

ANNOUNCER VO. Please stand back from the doors as the train approaches the Terminal

AGNES. Right on schedule

ANNOUNCER VO. Terminal

AGNES. Yeah, aren't we all?

ANNOUNCER VO. Do you hear me?

AGNES. I'm late

ANNOUNCER VO. Agnes?

(sound of train approaching)

AGNES. Three

ANNOUNCER VO. This is the Blue line, Eastbound

AGNES. Two

ANNOUNCER VO. Please stand back from the doors

AGNES. One

ANNOUNCER VO. Final stop, Darjeeling!

AGNES. OP!

*(Time suspends, **AGNES** flies, transforming into a bird, flaps into the sky.)*

(sky and birds)

(breaking glass and brakes screeching)

(empty spotlight on platform)

(Announcer and Dispatcher are overlapping in the chaos.)

DISPATCHER VO. All Blue Line trains Eastbound and Westbound, please hold until further notice! All Blue Line trains eastbound and westbound, please hold until further notice!

ANNOUNCER VO. All Blue Line traffic Eastbound and Westbound will be delayed indefinitely, please take alternate routes to your destination. All Blue Line traffic Eastbound and Westbound will be delayed indefinitely.

(Lights fade.)

23

b on Ella's apartment)

(Everything has stopped.)

(The window is shattered.)

(**SHIPKOV** *is sitting on top of the train looking directly at* **ELLA**.)

SHIPKOV. I've killed two people and one dog. You believe me? Hm?

I've killed two people and one dog in seven years.

Many drivers are lucky, they never have a jumper their whole career– but they seek me out. Like missiles. Like death-seeking missiles–

In Sofia I was a circus man. Twenty years with the Circus Arena, OPPA! BRAVO! DA! BRAVO! I was in charge! Of telling the audience what to think, how to feel, when to laugh... or scream. Twenty years, I never lost an artist! Twenty years and we had only small injuries to remind us to stay alive to pay attention, but we never lost one! Not one.

The first I killed was a man, a drunk. He fell on the tracks, it was late so no one saw him, and Glupak walks into the tunnel instead of climbing out. Or maybe he was too drunk to climb out, I don't know that. I saw him like a shadow, tipping around, doesn't even try to move out of the way. Trips and sits down on the track in front of me like he's going to tie his shoelace or something. OPPA! So, that was number one.

Number two was quick. Just as I came out of the tunnel he jumped. Had his eyes shut... I wanted to shout at him, 'Some people should just sell shoes! Eyes open!' OPPA! DA! Number two.

I was very angry about the dog. The dispatcher screwed up on that one. Word comes out on the speaker that this dog has run into the tunnels and they stop all the trains going West because that is the track he is on! But the idiot forgets that the tracks connect, East and West running side by side for several meters, and doesn't stop the trains going East, so the dog runs onto my track and OPPA! DA! Number three. I was very angry about that! About the dog. The dog wasn't trying to die. That was a big screw up!

DOCTOR VO. Mr. Shipkov? Mr. Shipkov? He's in shock. Can you hear me?

SHIPKOV. Now number four... number four was something else. I'll tell you something.

I had my eyes open, in that moment when it happened. And I saw. A bird flying away through the tunnel. Flying away.

Bravo! Da! What a thing, ah?

DOCTOR VO. Hello? Hello?

SHIPKOV. What a thing!

I look at people, and I want to say to them, think! Maybe you are ordinary? Maybe you should make buttons? Or sell shoes? Maybe you should break the law? Maybe you should talk big and invent a life that you would prefer? Fine.

But if you get in my way, I will kill you.

DOCTOR VO. Can you hear me, Mr. Shipkov?

SHIPKOV. They think I have a choice. I have no choice.

I will kill you.

DOCTOR VO. Ok, he's coming to. Mr. Shipkov! Can you open your eyes?

SHIPKOV. Of course. I am a circus man. I keep my eyes open

(**SHIPKOV** *smiles.*)

Oppa! Bravo! Da!

(*Blackout*)

24

(Lights fade up on **ELLA** *alone in the wreckage.)*

(Silence, but it is no longer as quiet a place as in the beginning.)

(After some time there is the sound of a solitary bird outside the broken window.)

*(***ELLA*** looks, sees nothing.)*

(Silence)

ELLA. Agnes?

(Lights fade.)

END OF PLAY

ALTERNATE ENDING

(This alternate ending may be used if **SHIPKOV** *is not positioned on top of the train for scene 23. It was created for the Long Wharf Theatre production.)*

23

SHIPKOV. I've killed two people and one dog. You believe me? Hm?

I've killed two people and one dog in seven years.

Many drivers are lucky, they never have a jumper their whole career– but they seek me out. Like missiles. Like death-seeking missiles–

In Sofia I was a circus man. Twenty years with the Circus Arena, OPPA! BRAVO! DA! BRAVO! I was in charge! Of telling the audience what to think, how to feel, when to laugh... or scream. Twenty years, I never lost an artist! Twenty years and we had only small injuries to remind us to stay alive to pay attention, but we never lost one! Not one.

The first I killed was a man, a drunk. He fell on the tracks, it was late so no one saw him, and Glupak walks into the tunnel instead of climbing out. Or maybe he was too drunk to climb out, I don't know that. I saw him like a shadow, tipping around, doesn't even try to move out of the way. Trips and sits down on the track in front of me like he's going to tie his shoelace or something. OPPA! So, that was number one.

Number two was a girl. That was quick. She was standing there, and just as I came out of the tunnel she jumped. She had her eyes shut... I wanted to shout at her, 'Some people should just sell shoes! Eyes open!' OPPA! DA! Number two.

I was very angry about number three. The dispatcher screwed up on that one. Word comes out on the speaker that a dog has run into the tunnels and they stop all the trains going West because that is the track he is on! But the idiot forgets that the tracks connect, East and West running side by side for several meters, and doesn't stop the trains going East, so the dog runs onto my track and OPPA! DA! Number three. I was very angry about that! About the dog. The dog wasn't trying to die. That was a big screw up!

Now number four... number four was something else. I'll tell you something.

I had my eyes open, in that moment when it happened. And I saw. A bird flying away through the tunnel. Flying away.

Bravo! Da! What a thing, ah?

What a thing!

I look at people, and I want to say to them, think! Maybe you are ordinary? Maybe you should make buttons? Or sell shoes? Maybe you should break the law? Maybe you should talk big and invent a life that you would prefer? Fine.

But if you get in my way, I will kill you.

They think I have a choice. I have no choice.

I will kill you.

Me? I am a circus man. I keep my eyes open

Oppa! Bravo! Da!

(Blackout)

24

(Lights fade up on **ELLA** *alone in the wreckage.)*

(Silence, but it is no longer as quiet a place as in the beginning.)

(After some time there is the sound of a solitary bird outside the broken window)

*(***ELLA** *looks, sees nothing)*

(Silence)

ELLA. Agnes?

(Lights fade.)

END OF PLAY